THE MIRROR OF CAGLIOSTRO

BY

ROBERT ARTHUR

British Library Cataloguing-in-Publication Data
A catalogue record for this book is available from the
British Library

CONTENTS

ROBERT ARTHUR, JR.

Robert Jay Arthur, Jr. was born at Fort Mills, Corregidor Island, the Philippines in 1909. Arthur's father was a lieutenant in the US Army, and he moved home frequently in his youth, attending a variety of different schools. Despite gaining entrance to West Point, he decided against following his father in to the military, and instead enrolled at the University of Michigan, where he gained a B.A. in English and an M. A. in Journalism.

After graduating, Arthur moved to New York City, and during the thirties his short stories were published in a range of magazines, such as *Wonder Stories, Amazing Stories, Argosy Weekly* and *Black Mask.*

THE MIRROR OF CAGLIOSTRO

Robert Arthur

London, 1910.

The girl's eyes were open. Her face, which had been so softly young, flushed with champagne and excitement, was a thing of horror now. Twisted with shock, contorted with the final spasm of life ejected from the body it had tenanted, her face was a mask of terror, frozen so until the rigor of sudden death should release its hold. Only then would her muscles relax and death be allowed to wipe away the transformation he had wrought.

Charles, Duke of Burchester, wiped his fingers delicately on a silk handkerchief. For a moment, looking down at the girl, Molly Blanchard, his eyes lighted with interest. Was it truly possible that in death the eyes photographed, as he had been told, the last object that sight registered?

He bent over the girl huddled on the crimson carpet of the small private dining-room of Chubb's Restaurant, and stared into the blue eyes that seemed to start from the contorted face. Then he sighed and straightened. It was, after all, a fairy tale. If the story had been true, her dead eyes should have mirrored two tiny, grinning skulls, one in each—for a skull had been the last thing she had seen in life. *His* skull.

But the blue eyes were cold and blank. He had seen in them reflection from one of the tapers that burned upon the table, still set with snowy linen and silver dishes from which they had dined.

He amended the thought. From which Molly had dined. Dined as she, poor lovely creature from some obscure group of actors, had never dined before. He had dined afterwards. She had dined upon food, but he had dined upon life.

He felt replete now. It was a pity he had not been able to restrain his impulse to kill. London was a city of infinite interest in this, the twentieth century. He should have planned on a prolonged stay, to explore it fully, but temptation had been too great, after so long an abstinence.

He moved swiftly now. The cheap necklace of glass beads, which the girl's mind had seen as rare diamonds, he allowed to remain about the throat where they glistened against the blue marks of strangling fingers. But he took his cloak from a hook and threw it over his shoulders. He retrieved his hat and let himself out of the door without a backward glance for the empty husk that lay upon the rug.

A waiter in red livery was coming down the hall, past the series of closed doors that led to the famous—and infamous— private dining-rooms of Chubb's. Charles stopped him.

'I leave,' he said. 'My friend—' he nodded toward the closed door—'wishes to be undisturbed so that she may compose herself. Please see to it.'

A coin slipped from one hand to the other, and the servitor, nodded.

'Very good, Sir,' he said. No titles and no names were used at Chubb's. They were, however, well known to both the proprietor and all the help. A pity.

Charles walked down the long corridor, down the steps which led to the street without imposing upon one the necessity of exposing himself to the view of the crowd in the dining-rooms below. As he let himself out, the eight-foot tall doorman, cloaked in crimson with a black shako upon his head—a sight more goggled at in these days by tourists from puritanical America than even Windsor Castle—raised a hand. A hansom cab arrived in place precisely on the moment that his steps carried him to the kerb.

Without looking back, Charles tossed a coin over his shoulder. The giant doorman casually retrieved it from the air as a dozen beggars and street loungers leaped futilely for it.

'Burchester House,' Charles said to the coachman.

He settled back to stare with hungry eyes upon this, the new London of which he had seen so little—and could have seen so much if he had not let himself be carried away by the soft sweet temptation of Molly Blanchard's life so that. . . .

But it was futile to dwell upon it. There would be other occasions. As they rolled through the dark streets he let himself relive the moment when he had placed the necklace about Molly's throat, telling her to look deep into his eyes. The heady delight of the instant when her trusting eyes had seen behind the mask of flesh which he now wore. The almost intolerable joy of her struggles.

He realized that the hansom had stopped. For how long had he been living again those delights, unaware? There was not, after all, infinity ahead of him yet. Pursuit would be hot after him soon, and he was as vulnerable now as a new-hatched chick.

He stepped from the cab and flung the driver money. Charles, still with the down of youth upon his pink and white cheeks, strolled with the gait of a man much older and more experienced into the great, three-storied stone mansion which was the London residence of the Burchesters.

Inside, someone came scurrying out of the shadows of the almost dark parlour.

'Charles, my son,' his mother began, in a voice that trembled.

'Later, mother,' he said sharply, and brushed past her. 'I am going to my studio. I will be occupied for some time.' He started up the stairs toward the tower room where he kept his paints and canvases. Behind him he heard his mother whimpering. He paid no heed. As he reached the second floor he increased his pace. It would not do to be late in getting back to his sanctuary.

An hour later, with his mother weeping outside his door and the men from Scotland Yard hammering on it, Charles, Duke of Burchester, flung himself from the casement window and jellied himself on the cobblestones below.

Paris, 1963.

The Musée des Antiquités Historiques was a small brick building, twisted out of shape by the pressure of time and its neighbours. It stood at the end of one of Paris's many obscure streets, so narrow and twisting that no driver of even the smallest car, entering one, could be sure of finding room enough to turn around to get out again.

Beyond the Musée flowed the Seine, and if the waters of the Seine gave off any glint of light this overcast day, the glint was wholly lost in passing through the grime that darkly frosted the windows of the office of the curator, Professor Henri Thibaut.

Thibaut himself was ancient enough to seem one of the museum's exhibits, rather than its curator. But his eyes still snapped, and he spoke with a swift crispness that strained Harry Langham's otherwise excellent understanding of French.

'Cagliostro?' Thibaut said, and the word seemed to uncoil from his lips like a tiny serpent of sound. 'Count Alexander

Cagliostro, self-styled. Born in 1743, died in 1795. A man of great controversy. By some denounced as a fraud. By others acclaimed as a miracle worker—a veritable magician. Ah yes, my young colleague from America, I have studied his life. Your information is entirely correct.'

'Good,' Harry Langham said. He smiled. At thirty-five he still seemed younger than his age, although a carefully acquired professorial manner helped counterbalance his youthful aspect.

'Frankly, sir,' he added, 'I had just about given up hope of getting any decent information about Cagliostro to make my summer in Europe worth while. I'm an associate professor of history at Boston College—my period is the 18th century—and I am working for my doctorate, you see. I have chosen Count Cagliostro as the subject for my thesis. This is my last day in France. Only last night I heard of you—heard that you yourself had once written a thesis on the life of Cagliostro. I'm here, hoping you will assist me.'

'Ah.' Thibaut took a cigarette from an ivory box and lit it. 'And from what viewpoint do you approach your subject? Do you propose to expose him as one of history's great frauds? Or will you credit him with powers bordering on the magical?'

'That's my problem.' Harry Langham said frankly. 'To play it safe I ought to call him a mountebank, a faker, a great charlatan. But I can't. I started thinking that, and now—now I believe that he may really have had mystic powers. His life is wrapped in such mystery—'

'And you wish to clarify the mystery?' Thibaut said, his tone sardonic. 'You will write your thesis about Cagliostro. You will win an advanced degree. You will get a promotion. You will make more salary. You will marry some attractive woman. All from the dusty remains of Cagliostro. N'est-ce pas?'

'Well—yes.' Harry Langham laughed, a bit uneasily. 'Cagliostro—thesis—promotion—money—marriage. Almost like an equation, isn't it?'

'It is indeed.' With a sudden motion, Thibaut ground out his cigarette. 'Except that the answer is wrong.'

'How do you mean?'

'Cagliostro can bring you only grief. Go back to America and erase the name of Cagliostro from your memory!'

'But Professor!' Harry reflected that the French became excited easily, and the thought made his tone amused. 'You yourself wrote a thesis about the man.'

'And destroyed it.' Thibaut sank back into his chair. 'Some things our world will not accept. The truth about Count Cagliostro is one of them.'

'But he's been dead for nearly two hundred years!'

'M'sieu Langham,' Thibaut said, reaching again for the cigarettes in the ivory box, 'Evil never dies. No, no. Do not answer. There is little I can do to help you. I destroyed my thesis and all my notes. However, if you should go to London—'

'I go there tomorrow,' Harry told him. 'I sail from Southampton in a week. I hope to find some material on Cagliostro in the British Museum.'

'You will find little of value,' the Frenchman said. 'To the British, Cagliostro was a charlatan. But attend. Seek in the old furniture shops for a plain desk with a hinged lid, the letter 'C' carved into it in ornate scrolls. Once it belonged to Cagliostro. Later it was acquired by one of the Dukes of Burchester. I have reason to believe that certain of Cagliostro's papers were hidden in a secret drawer in this desk and may possibly still be there.'

'A plain desk with a hinged lid, the letter "C" carved into it.' Harry Langham's expression was eager. 'That would be a find indeed. I certainly thank you, Professor Thibaut.'

The older man eyed him sadly.

'I still repeat my advice—tear up your thesis, forget the name. But you are young, you will not do it. Very well, I shall make one more suggestion. 'Go—now, today—to the Church of St. Martin.'

'St. Martin?'

'I will give you the address. Find the caretaker, give him ten new francs. Tell him you wish to see the tomb of Yvette Dulaine.'

'Yvette Dulaine?'

'She was buried there in 1780.'

'But I don't understand—I mean, what point is there in seeing the tomb of a girl who died in 1780?'

'I said she was buried then.' Thibaut's gaze was inscrutable. 'Insist that the caretaker open the tomb for you. Then do whatever you must do. Au revoir, my young friend.'

In the age-wracked Museum of Historic Antiquities, it had been easy to smile at the melodramatic earnestness of the French. Here, with the streets of Paris Lord alone knew how many feet above his head, moving down a narrow stone passageway slippery with seepage of water, holding aloft his own candle and following the flickering flame borne by the rheumatic old man in front of him, Harry found it less easy to smile.

They had gone down endless steps, along corridors that turned a dozen times. How old was this church anyway, and how far into the bowels of the earth did its subterranean crypts go? The whole thing was too much like an old movie for Harry Langham's taste. Except that the smell of damp corruption in the air, the shuffle of the old man's shoes on the rock flooring, and the scamper of rats in the darkness carried their own conviction.

They passed another room opening off the corridor, a room into which the bobbing candle flames sent just enough light to show old, elaborately carved stone tombs in close-joined ranks.

'Is this it?' Harry asked impatiently, as his guide paused. 'We must be there by now. We have had time enough to travel halfway across Paris.'

'Patience, my son.' The caretaker's tone was unhurried. 'Those who lie here cannot come to us. We must go to them.'

'Then let's hurry it up. This is my last day in Paris. I have a thousand things to tend to.'

They went on, around another turning, down some stairs and came into a low-ceilinged room dug from solid rock. The tombs here were simpler. Many had only a name and a date. In the light from the two candles, they lay like sleeping monsters of stone, jealously hiding within them the bones of the humans they had swallowed.

'Are we there at last?' Harry Langham's tone was ironic. 'Thank heaven for that! Now which of these dandy little one-room apartments belongs to Miss Yvette Dulaine? I've come this far. I'll see it, but then I'm heading back for fresh air.'

'None of these,' the caretaker said quietly. 'She lies over here, la pauvre petite. Come.'

He skirted the outer row of tombs and paused, lifting his candle high. In a crude niche in the stone a tomb apart from the others had been placed. It could have been no plainer—stone sides, a stone slab on top, the date 1780 cut into the top, no other inscription.

'She is here. It is only the second time in this century that she has been disturbed.'

Harry stared sceptically at the simple tomb. His shoes were damp and he felt chilled as well as somehow disappointed.

'Well?' he asked. 'What am I supposed to do? Say ooh and aah? Why isn't her name on it—just the date? How do I know this is even Yvette Dulaine's tomb?'

The caretaker straightened painfully. He held his candle up and stared into Harry's face.

'You are American,' he said. 'When this tomb was closed, your nation had but begun its destiny. You have much to learn.'

'Look,' Harry said, controlling his impatience with an effort. 'I agree we have a lot to learn. But I can't see I'm learning much here, looking at some chunks of stone that hide a lady who died one hundred and eighty-odd years ago.'

'Ah.' The other spoke gently. 'If she had but died.'

'If she had but—' Harry stared at him. 'What are you talking about? They don't bury you unless you're dead. Believe me, I know.'

'M'sieu's knowledge is no doubt formidable.' The other's tone was gentle, the sarcasm in his words. 'Let us now disturb the peace of Mlle Dulaine for but one moment more. We shall open her tomb.'

'Now really, that's hardly necessary—' Harry began, but stopped when the caretaker handed him his candle and grasped the bottom end of the slab top. He tugged; inch by inch the heavy stone moved, screeching its protest. Harry had no special desire to see some mouldering bones. He had avoided such a tourist attraction as the catacombs of Paris, just because he didn't care for morbid reminders of man's mortality. He liked his life—and death—in the pages of books. Both life and death were neat and tidy there and could be studied without emotion. He did not look into the open tomb until the caretaker straightened and motioned with his hand.

'Perceive,' he said. 'Look well upon the contents of this tomb, which the good fathers left nameless so that the poor one inside would not disturb the thoughts of the living.'

Still holding the candles, Harry bent over. As he did so, the flames flickered wildly, as if buffeted by drafts from all sides, though no breath of air stirred there. And the shadows they created made the girl in the tomb seem to smile, as if she would open her eyes and speak.

Her face was madonna-like in its perfection of ivory beauty. Heavy black tresses, unbound, flowed down upon her breast. Her hands, small and exquisite, were crossed upon her bosom. She wore something white and simple which exposed her wrists and arms. As he bent over her Harry's hand shook and one of the candles dropped a blob of molten wax upon her wrist. He so completely expected her to move, to cry out at the pain, that when she did not he felt a sudden wild rage. At her, for seeming so alive, so beautiful and so desirable. At Thibaut for sending him here on a fool's errand. At the shrivelled gnome of a caretaker for wasting his time on so childish a deception.

'Damn you!' he cried. She's a wax figure! What kind of tomfoolery is this?'

With surprising strength, the caretaker thrust the stone lid back into place. Harry had one last glimpse of the young and lovely face with the lips that seemed about to speak, and then it was gone. And he could not explain why he felt doubly cheated, doubly angered.

'So!' he shouted. 'You didn't want me to get another look! You knew I was going to touch her and see that she really was wax. Admit it and tell me why you bothered with this nonsense. Or is this a standard tourist attraction that you've rigged up to bring in a little income from gullible Americans?'

The Frenchman faced him with dignity, reaching for and taking back his candle.

'M'sieu,' he said. 'As I remarked, you are young, you have much to learn. Once, Mlle Dulaine attracted the attention of a certain Count Cagliostro. She refused him. He persisted. She rejected him utterly. One night she vanished from her home. The next day, servants of Count Cagliostro found her lying in his rooms, at the base of a great mirror as if she had been admiring herself. The Count was held blameless; he was far from Paris at the time.

'Mlle Dulaine seemed asleep, but did not waken. There was no mark on her. Yet she did not breathe and her heart did not beat. A week passed. A month. She remained unchanged. She did not begin that return to dust which is the fate of us all. So her sorrowing parents consigned her to the good fathers of the church, and they placed her here. She has remained as you see her, since the year 1780.'

'That's idiotic,' Harry said, shakily. 'Such things aren't possible. She's a wax figure. She's certainly not dead.'

'No, m'sieu. She is not dead. Yet she is not alive. She exists in some dark dimension it is not well to think of. The Count Cagliostro took his revenge upon her. She will sleep thus, until the very stones of Paris become dust around her. Now let us go. As you reminded me, you have many things to do.'

'Wait a minute. I want to see that girl—that figure—again.'

Harry's breathing was harsh in the silence; he felt his pulse pounding—with fury? with bafflement?—he couldn't tell what emotion he felt. But the caretaker was already moving toward the stairs.

In a moment he would be gone. Harry wanted to tear the stone slab off that tomb and satisfy himself. But to linger even a moment would mean to be lost in those Stygian depths without a guide.

Furious, he followed the flickering candle that was already becoming small in the darkness.

It was easy, in the daylight above, to regain his composure and laugh at himself for being tricked. It was easy, next day in London, when he met Bart Phillips, his closest friend at the university, who had spent the summer in London working toward his doctorate in chemistry, to entertain him with an elaborate account of the mummery he had gone through. It was easy to erase the lingering doubt that the girl had indeed been a wax figure.

Easy—until he found the mirror.

He found it in a dingy second-hand shop in Soho, called Bob's Odds and Ends. The desk he was seeking he had traced to an auction house which had suffered a fire. Presumably the desk had burned with many other rare pieces. But Bob's Odds and Ends had been mentioned in connection with the sale of the furnishings of Burchester House, residence of a ducal line now extinct.

Bob himself, five feet tall and four feet around the waist, did not bother to remove the toothpick from between his unusually bad teeth when Harry, with Bart in protesting tow, asked about the desk.

'No, guv'nor,' the untidy fat man said. 'No such article 'ere. Probably Murchison's got it, them wot 'ad the fire.'

'Come on, Harry,' Bart said. 'One last day in London and still you're dragging me to junk shops. Let's go get something to drink and see if we can't make a date with those girls from Charlestown we met.'

'Don't 'urry off, gents,' Bob said plaintively, unhooking fat thumbs from a greasy vest. 'Got somethin' pretty near as good. ' 'Ow would you like to buy th' mirror wot killed th' Duke of Burchester 'imself?'

'Mirror?' Harry asked, the word tugging at his memory.

'Come on, Harry!' Bart exploded, but Harry was already following the fat man toward the dark recesses of the shop.

The mirror was a tall, oval pier glass, hinged so that it could be adjusted. It stood in a corner. As the fat man swung it out, it rolled on a sloping stretch of floor, toppled sideways, and would have crashed down upon him if he had not sidestepped nimbly. The mirror fell to the floor with a violence that should have sent flying glass for a dozen feet.

The proprietor looked at it calmly, then heaved it upright.

'That's 'ow it killed th' duke,' he observed. 'Fell on 'im. And 'im with an 'atchet in his 'and, like he was trying to smash it. But this glass can't smash. Unbreakable, it is.'

'What's unbreakable?' Bart asked, following them.

'This mirror, according to the man,' Harry said.

'Nonsense. Glass can't be made unbreakable,' Bart said. 'Good Lord, it's all painted over with black paint. It's no earthly use to anyone. Come on, I'm dying of thirst.'

'But, gents, it's a rare mirror, it is,' the fat man said sadly. 'Without that paint, it'd be worth a pretty sum. Besides, it's an 'aunted mirror. It killed th' duke 'isself, and it stood in a closet for almost fifty years before that. Ever since th' duke's brother, wot was th' duke then, murdered a girl in Chubb's Restaurant back in 1910, then jumped out th' window into th' courtyard an' broke his neck when the bobbies came for 'im.'

'Come on, Harry,' Bart groaned. But Harry, on the verge of turning away, saw the faint glint of glass near the bottom where something sharp had scratched a few square inches of the black paint which covered the mirror's surface. It seemed to him the bit of glass reflected light, and he stooped to look into it.

He stared for a long minute, until Bart became alarmed and grabbed him by the shoulder.

'Harry!' he said. 'My God, man, you're the colour of putty. Are you sick?'

Harry Langham looked at him without seeing him.

'Bart,' he said, 'Bart—I saw a face in that mirror.'

'Of course you did. Your own.'

'No. I saw the face of that girl, Yvette Dulaine, who lies beneath St. Martin's Church in Paris. She was holding a candle, and looking out at me, and she tried to speak to me. I could read her lips. She said, "Sauvez-moi!" Save me!'

'What in God's name has happened to Harry Langham?' Bart Phillips demanded, and ran his fingers through bristling red hair. 'He's missed his classes two days in a row. Mrs. Graham, is he sick?'

The middle-aged woman, who might have stepped from one of the stiff portraits on the walls of the rundown Beacon Street house, compressed her lips.

'I don't know what has happened to him, Professor Phillips,' she said. 'He hasn't been himself for a week, not since he received word that mirror was due to be landed. Then since they delivered it two days ago he has not left his room. He makes me leave his meals outside the door. I have always considered Professor Langham a very fine lodger, but if this goes on—Well!'

She uttered the final exclamation to Bart Phillips's back as he took the broad, curving stairs of the once elegant house two at a time.

At the top, Bart hesitated outside Harry's door. Some dirty dishes sat on the floor just beside it. He tested the knob, found the door unlocked, and quietly pushed it open.

In the centre of the big, old-fashioned room, Harry was on his knees before the oval pier glass, laboriously scraping away at the black paint which covered its surface. From time to time he paused to wet a rag in turpentine, rub down the surface he had scraped, and then begin again.

The younger man walked quietly up behind him. The glass, he saw, was now nearly free of obscuring paint. It shone with an unusual clarity, giving the effect of a great depth. Then Harry saw his reflection and leaped up.

'Bart!' he shouted. 'What are you doing here? Why have you broken into my room?'

'Easy, boy, easy,' Bart said, putting a hand on his shoulder. 'What's the matter, are you in training for a nervous breakdown? I've been coming in your room without knocking for years.'

'Yes—yes, of course.'

Harry Langham rubbed his forehead wearily. 'Sorry, Bart, I'm edgy. Not enough sleep, I guess.'

Bart looked at the flecks of paint on the floor, and rapped the mirror with his knuckle. Harry started to protest, and subsided.

'At a guess,' Bart said, 'you have been working on this old looking-glass since it got here. Now honestly, Harry, aren't you being—well, illogical? I mean, you think you saw a girl's face mysteriously looking out at you from this mirror, back in London. You've been on pins and needles ever since waiting for it to arrive—you've hardly been over to see us, and I must say that Sis is hurt, since she kind of got the idea you planned to propose. Tell me the truth—are you expecting that girl is going to appear in this mirror again? Is that what you've had all along in the back of your mind?'

'I don't know.' Harry dropped into a chair and stared at himself in the mirror. 'I tell you, Bart—I just don't know. I feel I *have* to get this mirror clean again. Then—well, I don't know what. But I have to get it clean.'

'In other words, a neurotic compulsion,' Bart told him. 'Under an old church in Paris you saw a wax figure. Later your imagination played a trick on you—'

'It wasn't imagination!' Harry Langham leaped to his feet with a fury that astonished them both. 'I saw her. I tell you I saw her!'

He stopped, breathing harshly. His friend had fallen back a step in surprise.

'I—I'm sorry, Bart. Look, maybe I am being — unreasonable. Just let me get this mirror cleaned, and some sleep, and I'll be myself. And I'll come to dinner tomorrow night with you and Laura. How's that?'

'Well—all right,' Bart said. 'And you'll go to your classes Monday? I officially announced you had a virus, but I can't cover for you any more.'

'I'll be at my classes. And thanks, Bart.'

When Bart had left, Harry dropped into the chair again and stared at the gleaming mirror. It seemed to shine with a light which was not reflection, yet he could discover no source for it.

'Yvette!' he said. 'Yvette? Are you there? If you are—show yourself.'

He knew he was acting ridiculously. Yet he did not care. He wanted to see her face again—the face he had seen in a tomb in Paris, the face he had seen in a bit of mirror in London, the face he saw in his dreams now.

Nothing happened. After a long moment, he got to work again with scraper, turpentine and steel wool.

The paint stuck doggedly. Twilight had dimmed the room to semi-darkness by the time the glass finally showed no trace of black remaining.

Exhausted, Harry sank back into his chair and stared at it. It was curious how brilliant a reflection it gave. Even in the twilight it showed every detail of his room. His studio couch, his bookshelves, his pictures, his hi-fi set—they seemed three dimensional.

He sighed with fatigue and his vision blurred. The reflection in the mirror clouded like wind-rippled water. He rubbed his eyes and once again the image was clear. The handsome black-and-white striped wallpaper, the crystal chandelier for candles, the old rosewood harpsichord, the enormous Oriental rug on the floor, the hunting-scene tapestry on one wall—

Harry Langham sat up abruptly. The room in the mirror was a place he had never seen in his life. It bore no more resemblance to his own room than—than—

And then she entered.

She wore something simple—he had never had an eye for clothes, he only knew it was elegant and expensive and of a style two centuries old. Her black hair was bound up in coiled tiers. She carried a candle, and as she came towards him from one of the doorways that showed in the shadowy sides of the room, she paused to light the candelabra atop the harpsichord. Then she turned towards the man who was watching, his breathing quick and shallow, his pulse hammering. It was she. Yvette Dulaine, whose body lay buried beneath St. Martin's Church.

He thought she was going to step into the room with him. But she stopped as if at an invisible barrier, and gave him a glance of infinite beseechment. Her lips moved. He could hear no sound, but he could read the words.

'Sauvez moi! M'sieu, je vous implore. Sauvez-moi!'

'How?' he cried. 'Tell me how—'

She made a gesture of helpless distress. A ripple swept across the mirror and she was gone. Harry Langham sprang to his feet.

'Come back!' he shouted. 'Yvette, come back!'

Behind him the door opened. He turned in a fury, to see Mrs. Graham bearing a tray of food.

'What are you doing?' he shouted at her. 'Why did you break in? You sent her away! You frightened her!'

The woman drew herself up in starchy dignity.

'I am not accustomed to being spoken to that way, Professor Langham,' she said. 'I knocked, and heard you say "Come." I have brought your dinner. I would prefer that you arrange to lodge elsewhere as soon as this month is up.'

She set down the tray and marched like a grenadier out of the room.

Harry passed a hand hopelessly over his forehead. The sight of the food on the tray revolted him. He thrust it away and turned back to the mirror, which now was dull and lifeless in the almost darkened room.

'Yvette,' he whispered. 'Please! Please come back. Tell me how I can help you.'

The mirror did not change. He flung himself into the chair and stared at it as if the very intensity of his willing would make it light again, would reveal the strange and elegant room it had shown before. The room darkened, until he could no longer see the mirror. Then his fingers, gripping the arms of the chair, relaxed. Exhaustion overcame his willpower, and he slept.

It was the booming of a clock that woke him. Or was it a voice, speaking insistently in his ear? Or a sound as of a thousand tinkling chimes intermingled? Or all three? He opened his eyes, and saw before him the mirror, light emanating from it. Once again it showed the strange room. The candles in the crystal chandelier glittered. And an elegantly dressed gentleman, who leaned against the harpsichord and watched, smiled.

'You are awake, m'sieu,' he said, and now Harry heard the words clearly. 'That is good. I have been waiting to speak to you.'

Harry Langham rubbed his eyes, and sat up.

'Who are you?' he asked. 'Where is she? Yvette, I mean.'

'I am Count Lafontaine, at your service.' The man bowed. 'And Mademoiselle Dulaine will be here. She is waiting for you to join us. To save us.'

'Save you?'

'We are both victims of an evil done long ago, before even your great-grandfather was born. The evil of the most evil of living men, Count Alexander Cagliostro. But with your help, that evil can be undone.'

'How?' Harry demanded.

'In a moment I shall tell you. But here comes Mlle Dulaine. Will you not join us?'

Harry rose to his feet, feeling strangely light, disembodied.

'Join you?' he asked. And even as he spoke he was aware that his senses were dulled, his mind sleepy. 'Is it possible?'

'Just step forward.' The Count held out his hand. 'I will assist you.'

Beyond the man, Harry saw the girl come slowly into the room. She came toward him, slowly, on her face a look of infinite appeal.

'Yvette!' he cried. 'Yvette!' He took two steps forward, and felt his hand grasped by the cold, inhuman fingers of the man within the mirror. The pull but assisted his unthinking impulse. For a moment he felt like a swimmer breasting icy water, shoulder deep. Then the sensation was gone and he was within the room in the mirror.

He looked with exultation into the eyes of the girl.

'Yvette!' he said. 'I'm here. I'm here to save you.'

'Alas, m'sieu,' she said. 'Now you too have been trapped. Look.'

He turned. The Count Lafontaine bowed to him, formally.

'A thousand thanks, my young friend,' he said. 'It is half a century since last I left the world of the mirror. I am hungry for the taste of life again—very hungry.'

He kissed the tips of his fingers and flung the kiss to them.

'Adieu, mes enfants,' he said. 'Console each other in my absence.'

He strode confidently forward, and beyond him Harry saw, as through a window, his own room, dimly lit. The Frenchman stepped into the room and approached the chair where

Harry had been seated, and now the shadowed figure in the chair, which he had not noticed before, was suddenly clear and vivid.

'That's me!' he gasped. 'Yvette—that's me—asleep in the chair.'

She stood beside him, her coiled dark hair coming to his shoulders, and infinite regret tinged her voice.

'Your body, M'sieu Langham. *You* are here, in the world of the mirror, this dark dimension which is not life and is not death and yet partakes of both. In your sleep he spoke the words of his spell and evoked your spirit forth from your body without your awareness. Now he will inhabit your body—for an hour, a day, a decade, I do not know.'

'He?' Harry shook his head, fighting the sense of languor and oppression. 'But who is he? He said—'

'He is the Count Alexander Cagliostro, m'sieu. And see—he lives again, in your body.'

As they spoke, the figure that had emerged from the mirror world turned to smile at them with sardonic triumph. Then it settled down upon Harry's sleeping body, blended with it, vanished—and Harry saw himself rise, stretch and yawn and smile.

'Ah, it's good to be alive again, with a young body, a strong body.' It was his voice speaking and in English—his voice subtly accented.

'Now, au revoir. The night is still young.'

'No!' Harry flung himself forward—and was stopped by an impalpable barrier. The glass of the mirror—yet it did not feel like glass. It felt like an icy net which for an instant yielded, then gathered resistance and threw him back. 'You can't!' he cried. Come back!'

'But I can,' said Count Cagliostro reasonably, in Harry's own voice. 'And I shall come back when it pleases me. Meanwhile, it is best that none save myself should be able to see you.'

He raised his hand in the air and drew it downward, speaking a dozen words in rolling Latin. And Harry faced only darkness—an empty darkness that stretched beyond him, for an infinitude of time and space.

He lunged into it, and found himself spinning dizzily in a black void where there was neither substance nor direction. There was only a cube of light, from the mirror room, swiftly dwindling into a tiny gleam.

'Come back! You will be lost forever, m'sieu. I pray you, return!'

The words, faint and faraway, steadied his whirling senses. He saw the light, focused his thoughts on the room it represented, on the girl, and once more he stood beside her, with the candles flickering warmly above them and the hungry blackness behind him.

'Mon Dieu, I feared you were gone!' Her voice was unsteady. 'M'sieu, we are alone here together. Even the consolation of death and the sweet sleep of eternity is denied us. At least, let us keep each other company and take what comfort we may from that.'

'Yes, you're right.' Harry passed a trembling hand over his face. 'And maybe we'd better start with you telling me what in God's name has happened to us.'

It did not require many words, Harry thought dully, half stretched out upon a tapestried couch as he listened to the soft tone of Yvette's voice. She had rejected Cagliostro—and with a smile he had promised her that she would have all eternity in which to regret her decision. Then one night in her sleep a strange compulsion had taken her will, and she had gone to his home, admitted herself, and gone up to his empty room—to find him smiling at her from within the mirror. He had spoken—She had left her body behind crumpled on the floor—and she had joined him in the world of the mirror. Then he—his own body many miles away—had left her alone there until the time came for him to take final refuge himself in the world between life and death of which the mirror was a door that he had opened.

'But he died in 1795 in prison,' Harry protested.

'No, m'sieu. They but said he had died. His body is buried somewhere, as is mine, and like mine, it does not change. His spirit sought refuge here, in this sanctuary he planned long in advance. And from time to time he found means to escape, as he has now, in your body. Over the years, the crimes committed by various hands, yet all animated by the spirit of Cagliostro, would fill a library of horrors. One has heard of the Marquis de Sade. Yet the Marquis was but a man interested in things magical—until he encountered the mirror and met the gaze of Cagliostro. Then, m'sieu, the name of de Sade became synonymous with evil.

'Later, given but little choice, he assumed the flesh of a drunken servant who had entrée only to the lowest of London's dives. It was then he acquired a nickname which you will know. Jacques.'

'Jacques?'

'Jacques, the Ripper. Never was he caught, this Jacques. He froze to death in a gutter one winter night—but only after the spirit of Cagliostro had safely quitted his mortal flesh.

'And then young Charles, Duke of Burchester, acquired a desk and the mirror for his studio. And so fell into Cagliostro's power. But the evil Count was too greedy. The first night he killed a girl almost in public and must flee back to this, his place of safety. Charles, himself again, tried to break the mirror. When he could not, when the men of the police came for him, he covered the mirror with black paint, and then he threw himself from his window and was dashed to death on the stones below.

'Now, m'sieu—' her gaze was compassionate—'he is free again in your body. And the hunger is strong within him. I would speak words of consolation, but unfortunately I cannot.'

'But what is he doing?' Harry started to his feet. 'My God, Yvette, isn't there any way to know what he is up to and to stop him?'

'It is possible to know what he is doing,' she said at last, 'for the spirit still is connected with the body, though but faintly. But he cannot be stopped. He is the master, we are his prisoners. And it is not wise to know what your body does at his orders.'

'I must know, I have to know!' Harry declared feverishly.

'Then lie back, stare at the burning candles, and let your mind empty itself. . . .'

He was in a bar somewhere. A crowded, noisy, smoky dive. Impression of laughter, of voices. Of a face looking up into his. A hungry face, over-painted, yet still with some youthful sweetness in it not quite destroyed. They were moving. They were outdoors. They were strolling down a narrow street toward the waterfront, and light and sound here left behind.

The girl was petulant. She did not want to go. But he laughed, and with a hand on her elbow, urged her onward. They came to a railing, with the dark water swirling below, and a mist curling around them.

'No, I'll show you what I promised you,' he was saying. 'But first we must remove these.'

He deftly removed from her ears the cheap, dangling crystal earrings, dropped them into his pocket.

'Why did you do that?' Her voice was shrill, angry. 'You can't treat me like that.'

'Your beauty should be unadorned. Look into my eyes.'

She looked and her gaze grew fixed. In his eyes she saw the black void of eternity, and rising from it the grinning skull-face of Death. She did not struggle, did not scream as his hungry fingers closed around her throat. Only when it was too late did she fight, so deliciously, so rewardingly. When he dropped her over into the rolling waters below and saw them suck her down with hungry swiftness, he felt again deliciously warm and full. . . .

'M'sieu! M'sieu!'

He opened his eyes. Yvette was shaking him, her face concerned.

'M'sieu, you looked so distressed! I told you it was not wise—'

'I'm a murderer,' Harry groaned. 'I killed her—killed that girl for the sheer lust of killing. . . .'

'Comfort yourself, m'sieu. You did not. It was he, Cagliostro, slaking his hunger for life. It is thus his spirit feeds, grows

33

strong—on the life of those he sacrifices.'

'But it was my hands that choked her—Oh, my God, what are we going to do?'

He stood up, his hands clenched. 'Can't we do *anything?*'

'Nothing, alas. He lives—in your body. We are shadows of the spirit trapped between life and death. Someday he will return and you will once more regain your body—'

'To be accused of all the infamous crimes he committed!' Harry cried. 'To pay for them. But first, I'll break this mirror. That's one thing I won't fail to do.'

Her gaze was wistful.

'If only that could be. Then I could at last die and be at rest. But you will not do what you think. Others have tried and failed. This mirror cannot be broken by human hand—only he himself, Cagliostro, can break it. No—do not ask. I cannot answer how or why these things are. He has the knowledge. I have not. Now, you must distract yourself. Come—let me show you this world.'

He let her take his hand, and numbly followed as she led.

There were doorways to the great room, several of them. She led him through one and he found himself in a small, book-lined library, where alchemical apparatus crowded tables, and a small, white-globed lamp burned with a bright fierceness. A book lay open, revealing mystic symbols. A giant spider squatted upon it and stared at them with glistening pinpoint eyes.

'His library,' Yvette said. 'Once the mirror stood in this room in the world of reality. Everything in the mirror reflected since it was made exists in this dark and fathomless dimension, if only it was reflected long enough; and his arts can call it into being.'

'Like a time exposure being developed,' Harry muttered to himself.

'Pardon?'

'I was just thinking. What lies beyond?'

'There are many rooms and a garden and even a pond. I will show you.'

There were indeed other rooms, but Harry viewed them without interest. There was a garden where fruit trees bloomed, and a pool that reflected the sunlight of a sun not seen for two centuries. But when he would have gone on, through other doors, Yvette held him back.

'No, m'sieu. Beyond there is nothing. Darkness. Emptiness. Where one can become lost and wander until the end of time. And in the darkness there are—creatures.'

She shivered as she spoke the word. But Harry persisted in his exploration. He opened a closed door—and there beyond it did indeed lie abysmal darkness. There were sounds in the darkness . . . flutings and wailings like no sounds he had ever heard before. And something darker than darkness itself drifted past as they watched, accompanied by the sound of a myriad of tiny bells. Swiftly Yvette slammed the door.

'Please, m'sieu,' she panted. 'Promise me. Never go into the darkness. Even Cagliostro knows not what it is or what creatures inhabit it.'

'All right, Yvette,' Harry agreed. 'I promise. Let's go back. Maybe Cagliostro has returned. Maybe he'll be ready to give up my body now.'

They returned through rooms of a dozen different sorts, one of them plainly the cabin of a ship. In the room of the mirror, the candles still burned as they had before, unconsumed and eternal. The wall of blackness which was the mirror remained in place. But even as they entered it, it dissolved, became a window beyond which was Harry's study where Cagliostro sat at a table, eating breakfast and reading a newspaper.

He smiled smugly at them.

'I hope you have become well acquainted, mes enfants. I have waited for your return. M'sieu Langham, this body you have loaned me is a splendid one, so strong, so handsome, so indefatigable. I shall enjoy its use for a long time, I think. This time I make no foolish mistakes. I have begged the most humble pardon of Mrs. Graham, your good landlady, and she has forgiven me. This evening I dine with your friend, Bart, and his sister Laura, with whom I gather you have — what is the word? — an understanding. I must make amends to them for your behaviour.

'Ah, my good friend, this Boston of yours is a most interesting city. Cold and reserved in appearance, yet it has its undercurrent of wickedness quite as naughty as London or Paris. I enjoyed myself last night. I was rash, perhaps, but fortunately I escaped detection. And now my motto is to be—discretion.'

He rose and tossed down his napkin.

'Now, I shall rest,' he said, and yawned. 'Last night was—fatiguing. Tonight may be the same. Au 'voir.'

He swept his hand downward with a roll of unknown words, and blackness sprang into place.

Wretchedly, Harry turned to the girl.

'How long were we?' he asked. 'A dozen hours have passed since last night, but it seemed like only a few minutes—half an hour, perhaps.'

'There is no time here,' Yvette told him. 'An hour may seem a day, a day an hour. You will become used to it, M'sieu Harry. Compose yourself—think not of Cagliostro.'

She seated herself at the harpsichord and begun to play a light, tinkling tune to which she sang in a sweet soprano. Harry flung himself down on the tapestried couch and listened. Gradually he relaxed. His mind ceased to throb and burn with turbulent thoughts. But as it did, other images, other sounds and sensations entered it.

Voices. Bart and Laura. Laughter. Wine.

'It's good to see you acting normal again, Harry. You had us worried.'

'I don't wonder, old man. That mirror delusion—you brought me to my senses. Guess I worked too hard in Paris.'

'Then there wasn't any girl in the mirror?' Laura's voice. Laura's smile. Laura's hand lightly on his arm as her eyes begged for assurance.

'If there was, she looked like me and needed a shave.' Laughter. 'Besides, what good would a girl in a mirror be?' More laughter. 'You'll see for yourself. When we set up house-keeping.'

'Goodness. Is that a proposal? Or a proposition?' Wide, hopeful eyes, lips that hide a trembling eagerness.

'Look, you two—while you debate the question, I have to see a graduate student of mine who's working on an interesting line of experiment.' Bart, rising, leaving. 'I won't be back until late.'

'Tactful Bart.'

'A nice brother. I like him. Harry—'

'Yes?'

'Whether it was a proposal or a proposition, it's a little sudden. Since you got back from Europe, I've hardly seen you. Why, I think you've kissed me once.'

'An oversight I plead guilty to. I can only say I'm prepared to make amends. Like this.'

Warm lips. Tremulous response becoming breathless excitement.

'Harry! What *kind* of overwork did you do in Paris? What research were you engaged in, anyway?'

'Can not we go elsewhere? . . . This is better. My dear . . .'

Breathless excitement becoming recklessness.

'Harry! You mustn't!'

'Oh, yes, my dear I must.'

'And I thought you were so prim and proper—even though I liked you.'

'And I thought you the same. How wrong we can be about people! Now. . . .'

'Stop!' Harry leaped to his feet, pressing his fists to his forehead, shutting out the damnable sensations from his distant body.

'M'sieu Harry.' Yvette rose and came to him. Gently she touched his forehead. 'It is Cagliostro again. You must not try to know what it is he does.'

'I can't help it.' Harry groaned. 'My God, I never thought that Laura—'

'Do not speak of it. Shall I read to you? Shall we walk in the garden?'

'No, no . . . Yvette.'

'Yes?'

'Cagliostro controls whether or not we can see the world outside the mirror—and whether it can see us.'

'That is true. He has charms that control it. If he speaks but the words, we can see and be seen but not heard. Or hear, but not be seen. And the greatest charm, that of drawing the spirit from the body and transporting it within the mirror. Alas, m'sieu, I crave your pardon.'

'For what?'

'It was I—I who enticed you here. I could not help myself. Cagliostro worked magic that brought you to that shop in London where the mirror lay—he had waited long for the right moment. It was he who enabled you to see me. It was his doing that you determined you must own the mirror, must see me.'

'I did feel—possessed,' Harry admitted. 'But don't blame yourself, Yvette. Even without Cagliostro you would have attracted me.'

'You are gallant. I thank you.'

'But what I started to say, if Cagliostro has charms, we can learn. We are not entirely helpless.'

'Learn them? It is true, his books, his philtres, his mystic objects are within his study—'

But in the study, where the white-globed lamp burned with

an undying brilliance, Harry groaned and pushed away the strange books, the ancient parchments, after he had leafed through them.

'I can't read them. They're not Latin. Maybe Sanskrit. Maybe Sumerian. Maybe some language that died before history began.'

'It is true,' the girl told him, 'Cagliostro has said that his magic is older than history, that it comes from a race so ancient no trace is left.'

'And I don't believe in magic. That's one trouble. I belong to the twentieth century. Even here—even a victim of it—I still can't believe in magic!'

'Oui,' Yvette agreed, 'belief is necessary. Without belief, the magic does not work. But then one must have faith in God, as well as in evil, m'sieu.'

'Yes, of course!' His eyes lighted. 'And what is magic to one age is mere science to another. So why shouldn't science to one age be magic to another? Yvette, help me work this out.'

'Anything I can do, anything,' she said. 'Sometimes Cagliostro had me help him. He said that in things mystic the female principle helps. Wait.'

She took pins from her hair, let her tresses tumble down over her shoulder. From a drawer beneath the bookselves she withdrew an odious object—the dried and shrunken head of a man who once had had flaming red hair and a red beard.

She sat facing him, the head upon her lap.

'Now, m'sieu,' she said. 'This head—Cagliostro swore it was the head of one of the thieves crucified with the true Christ. Perhaps. But now I look like a sorceress. I will sit in silence, and you shall study.'

'Good girl!' He plunged anew into an effort to make sense of the books, the cabbalistic symbols. In his mind he thought of them as simply equations which produced certain results. So categorized, he was able to believe in them. After all, this mirror world—was it so much more than a photograph caught on celluloid, or a motion picture electronically impressed upon magnetic tape? Perhaps the people in pictures felt and thought!

And wasn't it Asimov, right here in Boston, who had said that some day the entire personality of a man could be put on tape, to remain forever, to be reproduced again whenever and as often as desired? What would existence inside a magnetized tape be? What thoughts would the man there think?

Perhaps his analogies were faulty, but they helped give him confidence. Yvette sat in silence as he worked, with feverish imtensity. He deciphered a word, a sentence, for Cagliostro had translated into a doggerel of Italian, French and Latin the older, unknown language—which might, after all, be the scientific language of a long dead race.

As Yvette had said, there was no time in this place. At intervals he paused and put his fingers to throbbing temples. Then he was aware of sensations from the world of life. His classrooms. Students listening with rapt intensity they had never paid before. Himself speaking with brilliant detail of life in London, in Paris, in the eighteenth century. A girl in the back row, blonde, with a face as soft as a camelia. A girl who paused after class at his request.

'Miss Lee, you are very silent. Yet I think you are hiding a genuine intelligence. Are you afraid of me?'

'Afraid of you? Oh professor, I couldn't ever be that.'

'You need confidence. You need—awareness. I would like to talk to you about yourself. Tonight?'

'Why—why, yes, professor.'

. . . Night. His car. Driving. Lights. Stopping.

'Professor. What—what are you doing?'

'Look into my eyes, child. You are not afraid of me?'

'I—I—no, I trust you. I trust you forever and always.'

'That is good. Now come.'

He forced his thoughts back to the books before him. He translated, worked out probable sequences, guessed where he had to. Still the awareness crept into his mind whenever he relaxed.

'Harry—I haven't seen you for so long.'

'Working on my new thesis, Laura. That fraud Cagliostro—

I've torn him up. The new one is to be a comparison of social life in London and Paris in the eighteenth century.'

'It sounds quite exciting.'

'It will be masterly. But I must make up for my neglect. My darling—'

'Harry! But—'

'No buts. Did you know that among the Romans—'

Doggedly he resumed work. But the outside impressions pressed in more strongly.

An alley. Blare of music. A girl, provocative in a red dress. She smiled into his eyes. . . . And lay cold, moments later, in a shadowed corner. . . . Another girl. Walking home from a bus. A scream. A struggle, sweet in its intensity. . . .

'No,' he groaned. 'No, Yvette! The things he is doing! The things *I* am doing! Even if I conquer him—I can't live. Not with what I have done.'

'Poor M'sieu Harry,' she said. 'But can you conquer him? Suppose you force him to return here and give back your body, what then? This mirror—it too is under a spell. It can be broken only by Cagliostro."

'Maybe,' Harry said grimly. 'But it hasn't been tested in an atomic explosion. In any case I'm pretty sure that, bathed in hydrofluoric aeid, it would dissolve. Or dropped into molten glass it too would melt.'

'But then—' Horror touched her features. 'But then I

would be lost forever in the darkness that lies outside, lost among the beings whose nature I know not. Only if the glass is broken is the spell broken. Only then can spirit and body reunite and blessedly find eternal sleep together.'

'I see. But Cagliostro must be removed from the world. If the mirror were dropped into the ocean where it is a mile deep. . . .'

She shuddered. But nodded.

'He must be removed, oui,' she said. 'What happens to me—it is not important. Continue, m'sieu.'

'I think I'm on the track.' He pronounced some words, crudely. "Does that sound familiar?'

'Yes!' her face lighted. 'It is what he speaks when he wishes to hear but not be seen. But it sounds like this—' She corrected his pronunciation. He repeated after her, the strange, rolling syllables.

'And this?' He spoke again, making a motion with his hand.

'When he wishes to see and be seen. Like this.' She corrected once more. 'And his hands—I'm not sure—there is a certain movement . . .'

He tried, but did no better. Then he stiffened. They heard voices. Real voices. For the first time.

'Yvette!' he whispered. 'We've won the first round. We can hear. Come, the other room. He is there, speaking to someone.'

They moved swiftly back to the great room where one wall of seething darkness represented the mirror. And words came through it.

'Professor Langham?'

'Associate Professor only, I'm afraid.'

'I'm Sergeant Burke, Homicide.'

'So Mrs Graham said. Homicide. Intriguing. What can I do for you, Sergeant?'

'Where were you at three this morning?'

'Here in my room. Working on my thesis. May I ask why you are interested?'

'A girl was strangled outside the Fishnet Bar last night.'

'I don't believe I've heard of the place.'

'One of your students was there. He believes he saw you with the girl who was killed.'

'I am a very ordinary type, Sergeant. And one of my students—in a bar at three in the morning? No wonder they learn so little—academically speaking, of course.'

'He described you pretty closely.'

'Perhaps because he has seen me in class for weeks. Let me assure you, Sergeant, based on their classwork, the powers of recognition and description of my students are limited.'

'Maybe so. Do you know a girl named Elsie Lou Lee?'

'Of course. One of my students. A shy thing.'

'She committed suicide last night. Cut her throat with a razor blade. Her last words were, "He said he wished I was dead and out of the way, so I'm going to die!"'

'A suggestible type, may I remark?'

'Her landlady describes you as the man who sometimes called for her.'

'Believe me, Sergeant, my description would fit twenty thousand men in Boston. I assure you I am too discreet to—fraternize—with a female student.'

'Yeah, I suppose so. But frankly—well, we've had eight women killed in this city in four months. Eight! All young, all without motive. I have to check out everybody.'

'Quite understandable.'

'So—I haven't any warrant—but if you'd be willing to come down and make a statement at Headquarters. . . .'

'With the greatest of pleasure. Let us go.'

Footsteps. A door closing. Silence.

'If only we'd had the rest of the charm,' Harry groaned. 'So that the Sergeant could have seen us! Then we'd have had him for sure.'

'He would have returned to the mirror,' Yvette said sadly. 'It is you who would have paid.'

'Even so—Let's keep trying. Tell me again what he said and

how he moved his hands.'

Repetition. Endless. Timeless. Then abruptly the curtain of black vanished and they saw, through the window of the mirror, into his room. In time to see the door open and Laura enter.

She looked distraught and haggard. She advanced swiftly, calling in case Harry might be in the bedroom.

'Harry! Harry, are you here? I must talk to you!'

'Laura!' Harry cried. 'Here. Here!'

She did not turn. She crossed the room, looked into the bedroom, then came and sat back on the studio couch, nervously pulling off her gloves.

'She does not hear,' Yvette said. 'There yet remains some part of the charm incorrect.'

'Laura!' Harry groaned. 'Please, for God's sake, look this way!'

She did not immediately look toward the mirror. But as she sat, nervously playing with her gloves, her gaze swept the room—and finally stopped upon the mirror. And then she saw them.

Slowly, unbelievingly, she rose to her feet and approached them.

'Harry?' she whispered. 'Harry?'

'Yes,' he said, then realized she could not hear. He nodded instead. 'Call the police!' He mouthed the words carefully but she stared at him with numb incomprehension. He turned to Yvette. 'Quickly!' he said. 'Paper and pen!'

Yvette ran. But before she returned, Harry saw himself enter the room. Cagliostro, as himself. And Laura, turning, stared from the man in the doorway to the image in the mirror with mounting disbelief and horror.

'Ah,' said Cagliostro, approaching her. 'Our friends have learned some tricks. I underestimated M'sieu Langham. Now you know.'

'Know what?' Laura asked huskily. 'Harry, I don't understand.'

'You will, my dear. Alas. My plans were so well made. Marriage, a long and honourable career on the faculty. Unlimited opportunities to indulge my little hobby unsuspected—all professors seem so harmless. Now it must end. But perhaps there is still a chance—'

'Laura, look out!' Harry shouted, futilely, Cagliostro approached her—and then his hands were around her throat, throwing her back across the bed, controlling her struggles until she lay still. Breathing hard, he rose. He looked into the mirror.

'Blame yourself, M'sieu Langham,' he said. 'But then, I was growing tired of her. A possessive type. If I can but get her to the river, it is possible I may yet bluff your stupid police into believing in my innocence.'

He turned and was drawing a blanket over Laura when the door burst open and Bart exploded into the room.

'Harry!' he shouted. 'Where's Laura? Mrs. Graham said she came up here. My God, man, don't you know you were seen with that Lee girl only last night before she—'

Abruptly he was silent, staring at the still figure only half concealed.

'Laura fainted, Bart,' Cagliostro said soothingly. 'If you will go for a doctor—'

'Murderer!' The words were a strangled sob as Bart flung himself at the other man. Cagliostro stepped aside and Bart sprawled on the bed atop his sister's body. Before he recovered, Cagliostro held a needle-sharp paperknife he had snatched from the desk.

'My young friend, he said suavely, 'usually I kill only women. But in your case I will make an exception.'

With the litheness of a fencer he came forward, the point extended. But he was unacquainted with the game called football. The younger man lunged low, caught him around the knees, and flung him backwards. His body stopped only because it came into contact with the face of the mirror. And a myriad of cracks streaked the glass to its every corner.

'The glass!' Yvette said in fervent joy, as she and Harry saw Cagliostro crumple forward, with the paperknife still in his hand. 'Cagliostro himself has broken it!'

Bart Phillips saw the cracked glass, and for just an instant he was aware of the two figures within the glass, figures already twisting and distorting as the glass came loose. A shower of a thousand sharp fragments fell across the prone man on the floor. In one fragment, Bart saw a single eye staring out at him. In another, a pair of lips murmured, 'Merci.'

Then the reflections were gone and the man on the floor groaned and with difficulty rolled over.

The paperknife emerged from his ribcase beside the heart, and dark blood stained his shirt and coat.

'Harry!' Bart dropped to his knee. 'Harry, *why, why?*'

'I am not your doltish friend Harry, m'sieu,' the dying man said. 'He is lost in some strange dimension where there is neither light, nor time, nor space.' His English now was accented. His features flowed, firmed. They became hook-nosed, sharp-jawed, the features of a man of middle age who has seen far too much of life.

'I am Count Alexander Cagliostro.' The words came with difficulty and were punctuated with blood issuing from the mouth. 'And I go now, his body mine, to meet the death which has awaited me patiently for almost two hundred years.'

He fell back, limp, and in a space of seconds his skin became a loathsome corruption, his hair powdered, and the white bone showed through. The corruption became horror, the horror dried, became dust, and the very bones beneath it melted like wax, falling in upon themselves. A moment later and there were but fragments mixed with dust.

www.ingramcontent.com/pod-product-compliance
Lightning Source LLC
Chambersburg PA
CBHW030530260626
47157CB00005B/1962